Newport Elem Sch Lib

P9-AOV-098

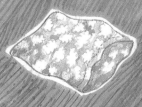

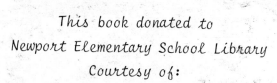

This book donated to
Newport Elementary School Library
Courtesy of:

**CHANNEL 33, WITF - TV**

MAY       1994

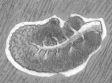

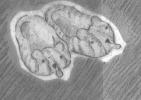

*For Lindsay with love,*
*and in memory of Rabbit*
AC & JB

Text copyright © 1990 by Alison Campbell & Julia Barton
Illustrations copyright © 1990 by Gill Scriven
First published in Great Britain by William Collins Sons & Co. Ltd.
All rights reserved. No part of this book may be reproduced or utilized in any form or by any
means, electronic or mechanical, including photocopying, recording or by any information
storage and retrieval system, without permission in writing from the Publisher. Inquiries
should be addressed to Lothrop, Lee & Shepard Books, a division of William Morrow &
Company, Inc., 105 Madison Avenue, New York, New York 10016.

First U.S. edition  1  2  3  4  5  6  7  8  9  10

Library of Congress Cataloging in Publication Data
Campbell, Alison. Are you asleep, Rabbit? / by Alison Campbell and Julia Barton;
illustrated by Gill Scriven.
p.    cm.     Summary: Donald has trouble getting to sleep at bedtime because he needs to
keep checking on the rabbit he has brought in from outside. ISBN 0-688-09490-2. — ISBN
0-688-09491-0 (lib. bdg.)   [1. Rabbits—Fiction.   2. Bedtime—Fiction.]   I. Barton, Julia.
II. Scriven, Gill, ill.   III. Title. PZ7.C1506Ar  1990      [E]—dc20      89-12974 CIP AC

Printed and bound in Belgium

# Are You Asleep, Rabbit?

*ALISON CAMPBELL & JULIA BARTON*
· Illustrations by Gill Scriven ·

Lothrop, Lee & Shepard Books
New York

One day it snowed.

"It's very cold, Rabbit. You'd better come inside," said Donald.

He carried Rabbit inside.

"Now you'll be nice and warm," he said.
Rabbit was so excited, she leaped down and
jumped round and round the kitchen.

"What would you like to eat, Rabbit?" said Donald. "You can't eat the wallpaper," and he gave her a carrot and some cabbage leaves instead.

"Where are you going to sleep, Rabbit?" said Donald. "No, you can't sleep in my boot," and he found some newspapers and a grocery box for a bed.

"It's time for bed, Rabbit. You must be tired," said Donald and he put her into the box.

Donald blew Rabbit a good-night kiss. Then he
closed the door gently and crept up to bed.

But Donald could not sleep.
  "Does Rabbit want a story?"
he thought.

He tiptoed downstairs with his book about
a big red fire engine.

"Are you asleep, Rabbit?" said Donald.
But Donald could not see Rabbit.
Then something tickled his toes.
   "Rabbit, what are you doing out
of bed?" he said.

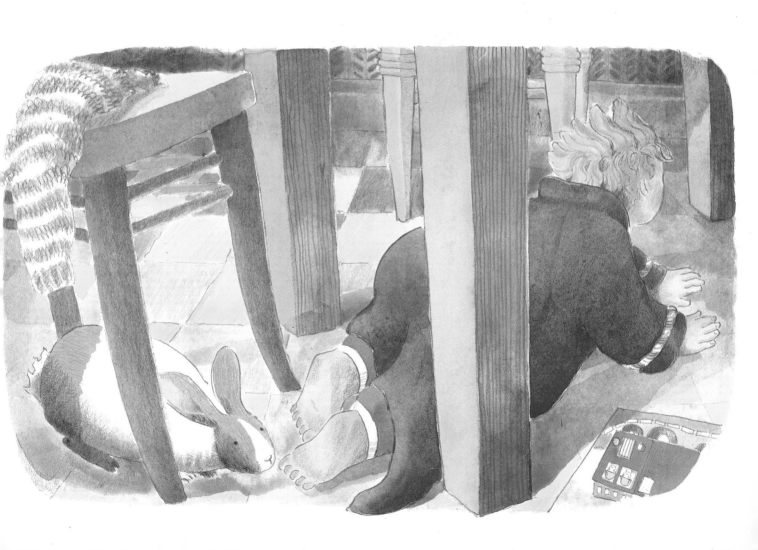

They sat down together and he showed
Rabbit the pictures and told her the story.
   He closed the book.
   "That's the end, Rabbit," said Donald.
"Now you must go to sleep."
   He stroked Rabbit's ears, then he went up to bed.

But Donald could not sleep. "Is Rabbit cold?" he thought.

He crept downstairs with his fluffy pink blanket.

"Are you asleep, Rabbit?" he said.
    But Rabbit wasn't asleep. She was dancing in
and out of the table legs.

"All right, Rabbit, just one dance. Then you really must go to bed," said Donald.
  And they danced a midnight dance.

Hoppity skip past the sink.

Hoppity skip round the vegetable rack.

Hoppity jump
over the broom
until . . .

they were so tired
they had to stop.

"You must be sleepy
now, Rabbit," said
Donald.

He said goodnight again
and tiptoed up to bed.

But Donald could not sleep.
"Does Rabbit want a drink?"
he thought.

Donald filled his shiny green mug with
water to take downstairs to Rabbit.

"Are you asleep, Rabbit?" said Donald.
But Rabbit wasn't asleep. She was under
the sink nibbling a box of soap powder.
"Rabbit! don't eat that!" said Donald.

"Look, I've brought you a drink," he said.
Rabbit woffled her little white nose and
lapped up all the water.

"Night night. No more tricks, now, or you'll be
too tired to wake up in the morning," said Donald.
He closed the door softly.

But Donald still could not sleep.
Mommy was asleep.
Teddy was asleep.
Horse was asleep.
Robot was asleep. But . . .

"Is Rabbit asleep?" thought Donald.

He put on his yellow
tiger slippers and
carried his softest
pillow down
to Rabbit.

"Are you asleep, Rabbit?" said Donald.
But Rabbit still wasn't asleep.

   The refrigerator door was open and Rabbit
was eating the tomatoes.

   "Oh Rabbit, I can't leave you alone at all,
can I?" said Donald.

He made a bed under the table with the fluffy blanket and the pillow. Then he picked Rabbit up gently and tucked her in beside him.

"Now I'll be able to keep an eye on you, Rabbit," said Donald.

He stroked her ears over and over until she closed her eyes.

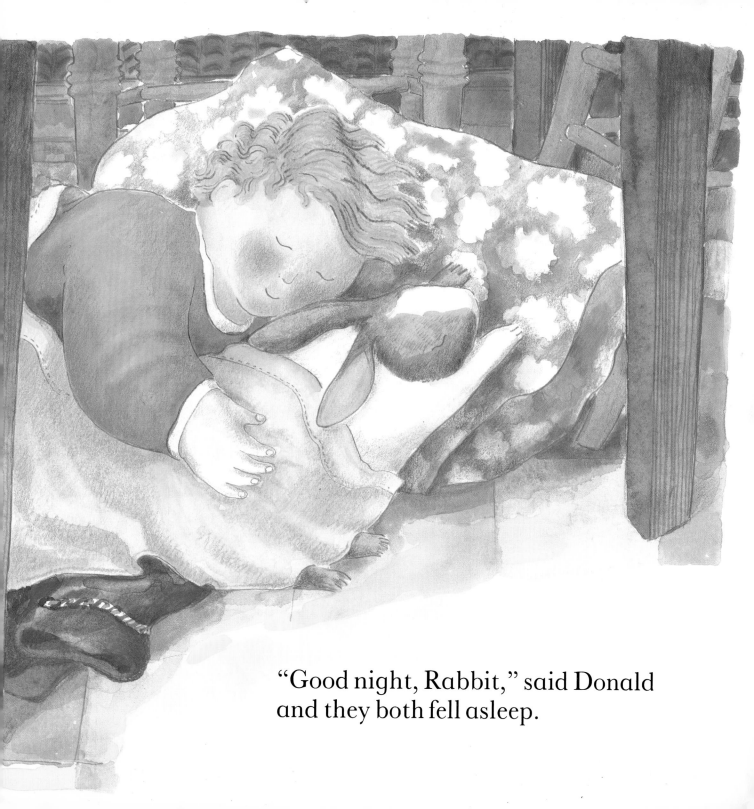

"Good night, Rabbit," said Donald
and they both fell asleep.